# BUFFALO

American Indian Legends Retold by Tiffany Midge
Additional Text & Book Design by Vic Warren
Illustrations by Diana Magnuson

## SCHOLASTIC INC.

New York  Toronto  London  Auckland  Sydney

The tradition of American Indian storytelling is older than history. Stories of the animals of North America have, for thousands of years, taught youngsters to honor and respect all forms of life. The authors are proud to bring this art form to the pages of this book, in the hope that we may entertain, educate, and inspire a new generation of children.

We wish to extend our special thanks to the Wichita nation for giving us their kind permission to retell *The Coming of the Buffalo*. We also wish to thank the Omaha, Seneca, Apache, Kiowa, and Ojibwa nations for their stories.

Additional thanks are due D. L. Birchfield for his technical assistance; the Philbrook Museum of Art, Tulsa, OK, for photos of the painted elk hide and the wooden

No part of this publication may be reproduced in whole or in part, or stored in a retrieval system, or transmitted in any form or by any means, electronic, mechanical, photocopying, recording, or otherwise, without written permission of the publisher. For information regarding permission, write to Scholastic Inc., 555 Broadway, New York, NY 10012.

Copyright © 1995 by Turning Heads, Inc.
All rights reserved. Published by Scholastic Inc.

**Library of Congress Cataloging-in-Publication Data**

Midge, Tiffany.
    Animal lore & legend — buffalo / American Indian legends / retold by Tiffany Midge ; additional text & book design by Vic Warren ; illustrations by Diana Magnuson.
        p.   cm.
    Summary: Includes both factual information and Indian legends about the buffalo or American bison.
    ISBN 0-590-22489-1
    1. Indians of North America — Folklore. 2. American bison —Folklore. 3. American bison — Juvenile literature. 4. Tales — North America. [1. Bison — Folklore. 2. Indians of North America — Folklore. 3. Bison.] I. Midge, Tiffany, 1965- . II. Warren, Vic, 1943- . III. Magnuson, Diana, ill., 1947- . IV. Title: Animal lore & legend — buffalo.
E98.F6M53 1995
398.24'5297358—dc20                           94-44267
[E]                                        CIP
                                            AC

12 11 10 9 8 7 6 5 4 3 2 1          5 6 7 8 9/9 0/0

Printed in the U.S.A.                            09

First Scholastic printing, October 1995

buffalo effigy; the Southwest Museum, Los Angeles, CA, for the photo of a Blackfeet summer camp, CT.313; and the National Museum of American Art, Smithsonian Institution, Washington DC/Art Resource, NY, for the painting by George Catlin of the Mandan Bull Dance.

Tiffany Midge is a Hunkpapa Sioux poet and writer whose work has been published in a variety of magazines, journals, and anthologies. In 1994, she was the recipient of the Diane Decorah Memorial Poetry Award from the Native Writers' Circle of the Americas for her collection *Outlaws, Renegades & Saints*, which is to be published by Greenfield Review Press. *Animal Lore & Legend—Buffalo* is her first children's book.

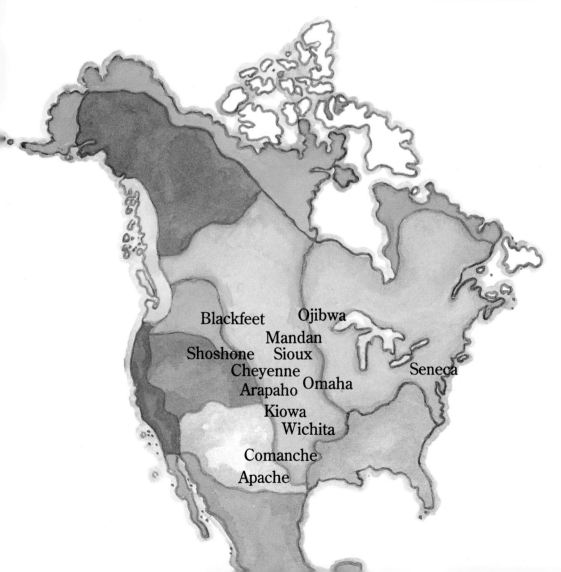

Blackfeet     Ojibwa
        Mandan
Shoshone    Sioux
    Cheyenne        Seneca
    Arapaho  Omaha
      Kiowa
        Wichita
    Comanche
    Apache

The buffalo is the biggest animal
in North America.
It is a mammal with horns, hooves,
and a large hump on its back.

Its true name is not buffalo.
It is American Bison.

Like cattle, buffalo are called bulls,
cows, and calves.

Once buffalo lived all across the Great
Plains and the Eastern Woodlands.

There were more than 60 million
buffalo in 1800.

Just 100 years later there were fewer
than 1,000!

Settlers and hunters killed them all.
Buffalo almost became extinct.

# THE BUFFALO AND THE GRIZZLY BEAR

From the Omaha and Seneca Stories

"Grr-rrr, grr-rrr!" Bear growled.

He felt mean and cross.
"I do not like anyone today," said Bear.

"I do not like Bobcat.
I do not like Wolf.
I do not like Badger!" Bear said.

"But I do not like Buffalo most of all!
Grr-rrr, grr-rrr!" Bear growled.

Bear came upon the river to get
a drink of water.

"Look at these fish!" Bear said.
"Grr-rrr, grr-rrr!" growled Bear.
"You fish better get out of my way!"

And all the fish swam away.
They did not like Bear, either.

"Grr-rrr, grr-rrr!"

Down the river, Buffalo was drinking.

The fish said, "Bear is mad, watch out!"

Bear saw Buffalo drinking at the river.
"What are you doing at my river?"
Bear said. "You better leave!"

"You do not scare me," Buffalo said.

Bear grew more angry.
"Grr-rrr, grr-rrr!"

Bear snarled, "I will eat you up!"

Buffalo said, "My, my, you are cross!"

Bear hit Buffalo on the nose with his
big paw.
"Take that!" Bear said.

"I do not want to fight," Buffalo said.

Bear hit Buffalo again on the nose.

"Ouch!" said Buffalo. "Let me be!"

"Grr-rrr, grr-rrr!" Bear growled.
And he hit Buffalo again.

Now Buffalo got mad and charged
Bear with his sharp horns.
He sent Bear flying through the air.

Bear fell hard on the ground. "Ooof!"

"Do you want to hit me now, Bear?"
Buffalo said.

"Weep, weep," Bear cried.

"Stop crying, Bear," Buffalo said.

"Can we be friends?" said Bear.

"Of course!" said Buffalo.

And Bear and Buffalo are now friends.

Cows and calves live in herds.
There are 20 to 50 buffalo in a herd.

Bulls live alone or with other bulls.
They visit the herds at mating season.

Buffalo bulls fight during mating season.

Bulls weigh up to 2,000 pounds.
They are about seven feet tall.
Big bulls can have horns two feet long.

Cows are much smaller.
They weigh about 1,000 pounds.
They are only four to five feet tall.
They have smaller horns than bulls.

Buffalo eat wild grass and grain.
They live and feed in large areas
called ranges.

Buffalo calves nap in the sun.

Buffalo calves learn to stand
and walk right after they are born.
They must move with the herd.
Calves stay in the center of the herd.
The cows protect the calves.

Southwest Buffalo Drawing

# THE COMING OF THE BUFFALO

From the Wichita, Apache, and
Kiowa Stories

Little Blue Sky and his people were
hungry, for the world was new and there
was nothing to eat but wild seeds.

"I wish we had some meat,"
said Sister.

"Yes," said Father.
"That would be good."

"What can we do?" asked Mother.

Everyone was hungry.
Something had to be done.

One day while Little Blue Sky was hunting for wild seeds he saw Raven. Little Blue Sky could see that Raven was very fat and had plenty to eat.

"I wonder where Raven hunts for his food?" Little Blue Sky said to himself. "I will follow him and find out."

And so he did.

But first he called out,
"Creator!  Use your power.
Change me into a puppy.
I want to find where Raven hunts!"

A strong wind blew from the north,
and the leaves on all the trees shook.

Then Little Blue Sky looked down
at his paws.
He wagged his curly white tail.
And he ran very fast to follow
after Raven.

Raven flew high.
His wings touched the sun.
He rested on a cloud and sang his
shrill song, "Caw caw caw!"

"Is this where Raven hunts?"
wondered Puppy.

Then Raven flew to the top of a big hill.
He looked all around. "Caw caw caw!"

"Does Raven hunt on the hill?"
wondered Puppy.

Raven went to a big flat rock.
He lifted the rock,
and a great buffalo ran out.
Raven chased the buffalo far away.

"Ahh," said Puppy,
"I have found where Raven hunts."

Puppy was very happy.
He ran to the rock and saw a big hole.
Puppy jumped down into the hole.

Down below was a world of
green grass, of high blue hills,
and all kinds of trees.
Puppy saw streams and lakes where
many buffalo had come to drink.

A young buffalo calf saw Puppy and
ran toward him.

"I have not seen you before.
Where do you come from?"
he asked Puppy.

"I come from above," Puppy said.
"Where all the people are."

The buffalo calf laughed.
"I do not believe you," he said.

"Follow me and I will show you,"
said Puppy.

The young buffalo calf called out
to all the other buffalo, "Follow me!"
And all the buffalo rushed
through the hole.

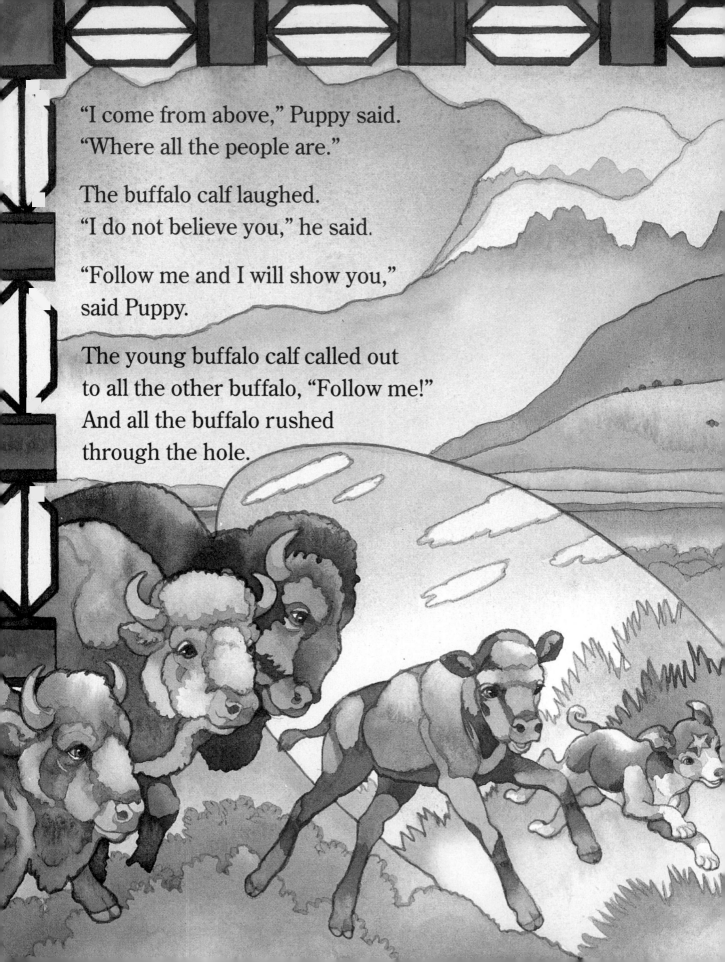

Their hooves made a big noise
like thunder.

Puppy turned back into Little Blue Sky.

He told the buffalo,
"This is the grass for you to eat.
And this is where you will live.
You are here so that all my people will
have food to eat."

And all the buffalo stayed to this day.

The Plains Indians hunted buffalo. They did not kill very many.

Indian hunters once hunted buffalo on foot.

They learned to be very quiet when hunting buffalo. It was very hard work.

Hunting became much easier when Indians learned to use horses and guns brought to North America by Europeans.

Shoshone Painted Hide

Blackfeet Tepees

Indians used all the parts of the buffalo they killed.

They made trail food called pemmican. It was made with dried buffalo meat and berries.

Old style Plains Indian homes are called tepees.
Once, they were made of buffalo hide hung on wooden poles.

Buffalo robes made warm beds and clothing in the cold Plains winters.
Rawhide is soft leather made from buffalo skin.
Moccasins, saddles, and even boats were made of rawhide.

Sioux or Cheyenne
Buffalo Carving

# WHY BUFFALO HAS A HUMP

From the Ojibwa and Seneca Stories

Buffalo have humps.
They hang their heads low.

And do you know why?

A long time ago,
Little Buffalo Calf liked to
run and jump and play.
Just like you do.

His father, the Buffalo Chief, said,
"You can run and play
in the green grass.
You can run by the stream.
You can run near the big trees.
You can run by the gray rocks.
But do not run near the
brown grass."

One day Little Buffalo Calf asked,
"Father, the brown grass looks nice.
May I play in the brown grass, please?"

"No," said the Buffalo Chief.
"You must keep out of the
brown grass."

"But why?" asked Little Buffalo Calf.

"Because that is where the birds live,"
said his father.

Little Buffalo Calf wished
he could play in the brown grass.

"I do not think the birds will mind,"
he said to himself.

When his father was not looking,
Little Buffalo Calf ran in the
brown grass.
He trampled the birds' nests
under his heavy feet.

The birds began to cry.
"You are a bad buffalo!" said the birds.
"You have ruined our homes!"

"Oh, my!" said Little Buffalo Calf.
He was sad.

Just then the Creator came.
"Little Buffalo Calf, you did not mind
your father," the Creator said.

"And now the birds have no home.
You must be taught a lesson."

The Creator put a stick on
Little Buffalo Calf's shoulders.
And there a big hump grew.

"I am sorry," said Little Buffalo Calf.
And he hung his head low with shame.

Now all buffalo have humps.
And they hang their heads low.

Today buffalo are
still endangered animals.
They have been protected for years.
There are more than 50,000 today.

Grizzly bears, wolves, and coyotes
used to prey upon the buffalo.
Today no grizzly bears or wolves are
left on the Great Plains.
Many coyotes are still there.

Once, the Plains Indians owed their lives to the buffalo. It fed and clothed them. Its skin covered their homes. Its bones made their tools. Even its tail was used to brush flies away.

Today, life in the Great Plains is very different. The spirit of Buffalo is still very important. Many Indian dances are ways of giving thanks for the buffalo.

Mandan Bull Buffalo Dance

# GLOSSARY

**Apache** (a-patch´-ee): An Indian nation of the desert Southwest

**Creator** (cree-ay´-tor): The maker of people, animals, and all other things in many Indian religions

**Extinct:** Not living now

**Endangered** (en´-dayn-jurd): In danger; a word used for animals and plants that are almost extinct

**Mating Season:** The time of year when animals breed

**Mammal:** An animal with hair or fur that has living babies, not eggs

**Moccasins:** Shoes made with pieces of rawhide sewn together

**Ojibwa** (oh-jib´-wa): An Indian nation of the Great Lakes region

**Plains Indians:** Indian nations of the Great Plains, such as Arapaho (uh-rap´-a-hoe), Blackfeet, Cheyenne (shy´-ann), Comanche (co-man´-chee), Kiowa (ky´-o-wah), Mandan, Omaha (oh´-ma-ha), Sioux (soo), and Wichita (witch´-i-ta)

**Prey** (pray): To kill and eat an animal

**Seneca** (sen´-a-ca): One of the six Iroquois nations of the Eastern Woodlands

**Shoshone** (sho-sho´-nee): An Indian nation of the Rocky Mountains